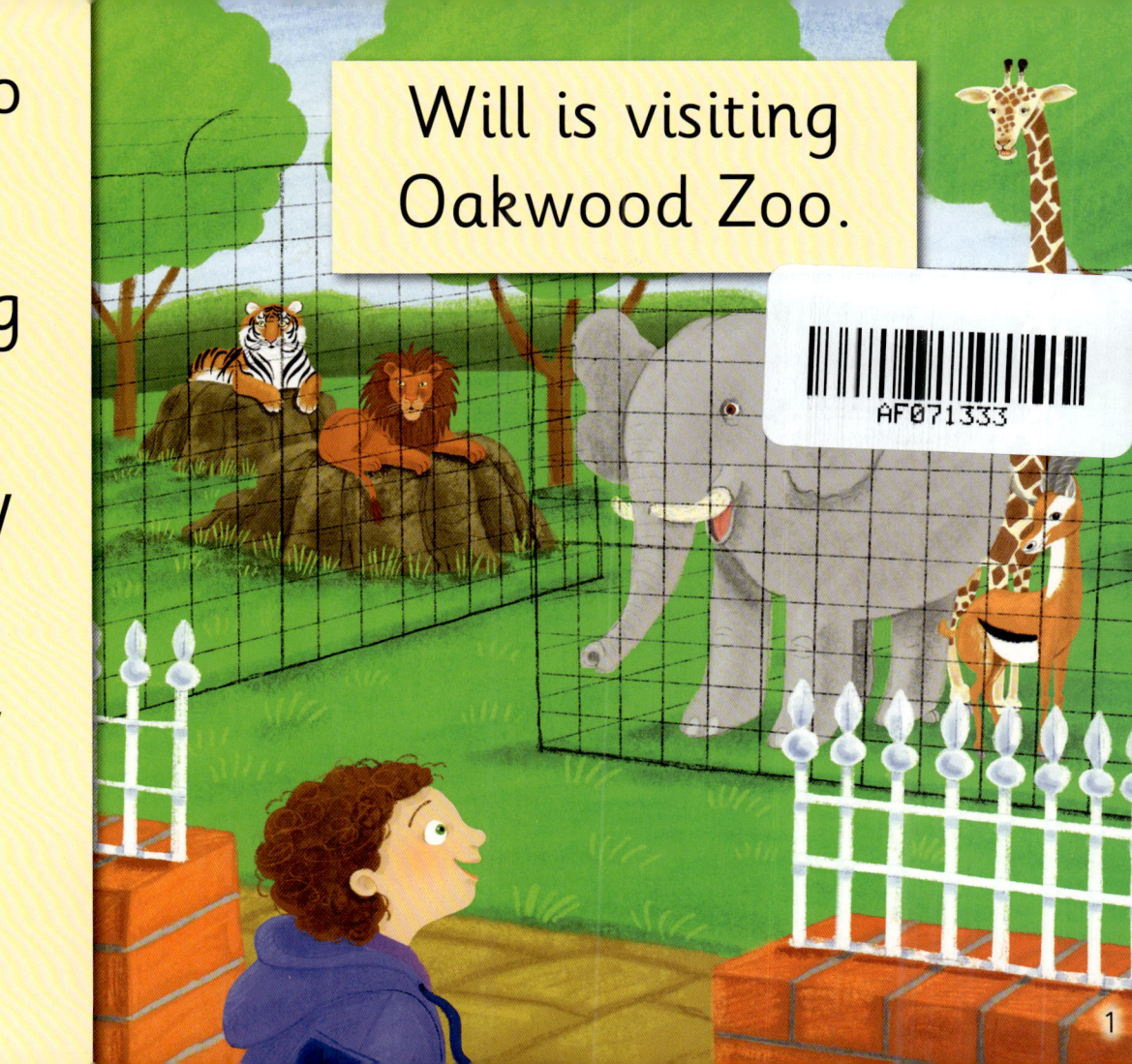

Will is visiting Oakwood Zoo.

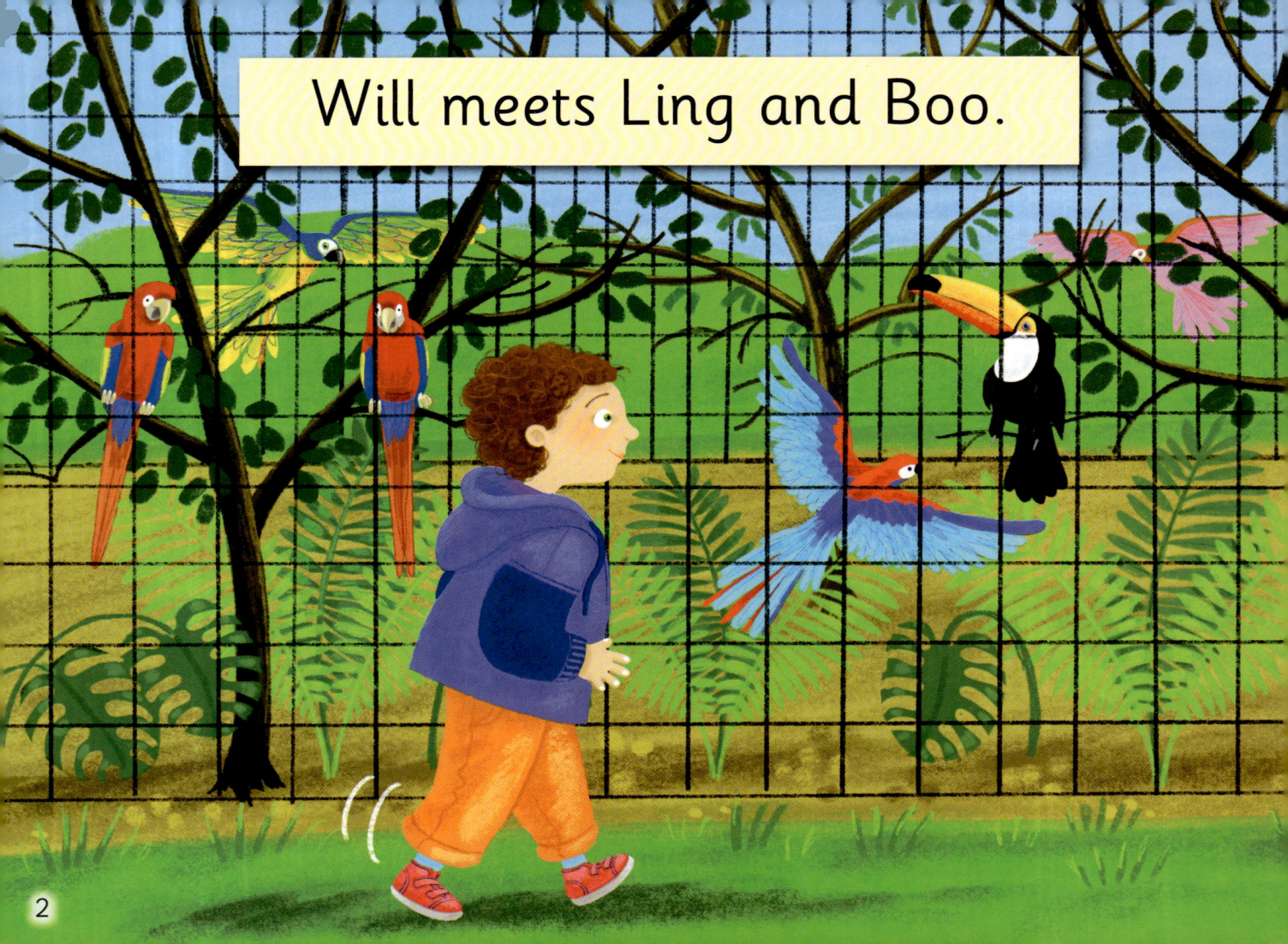

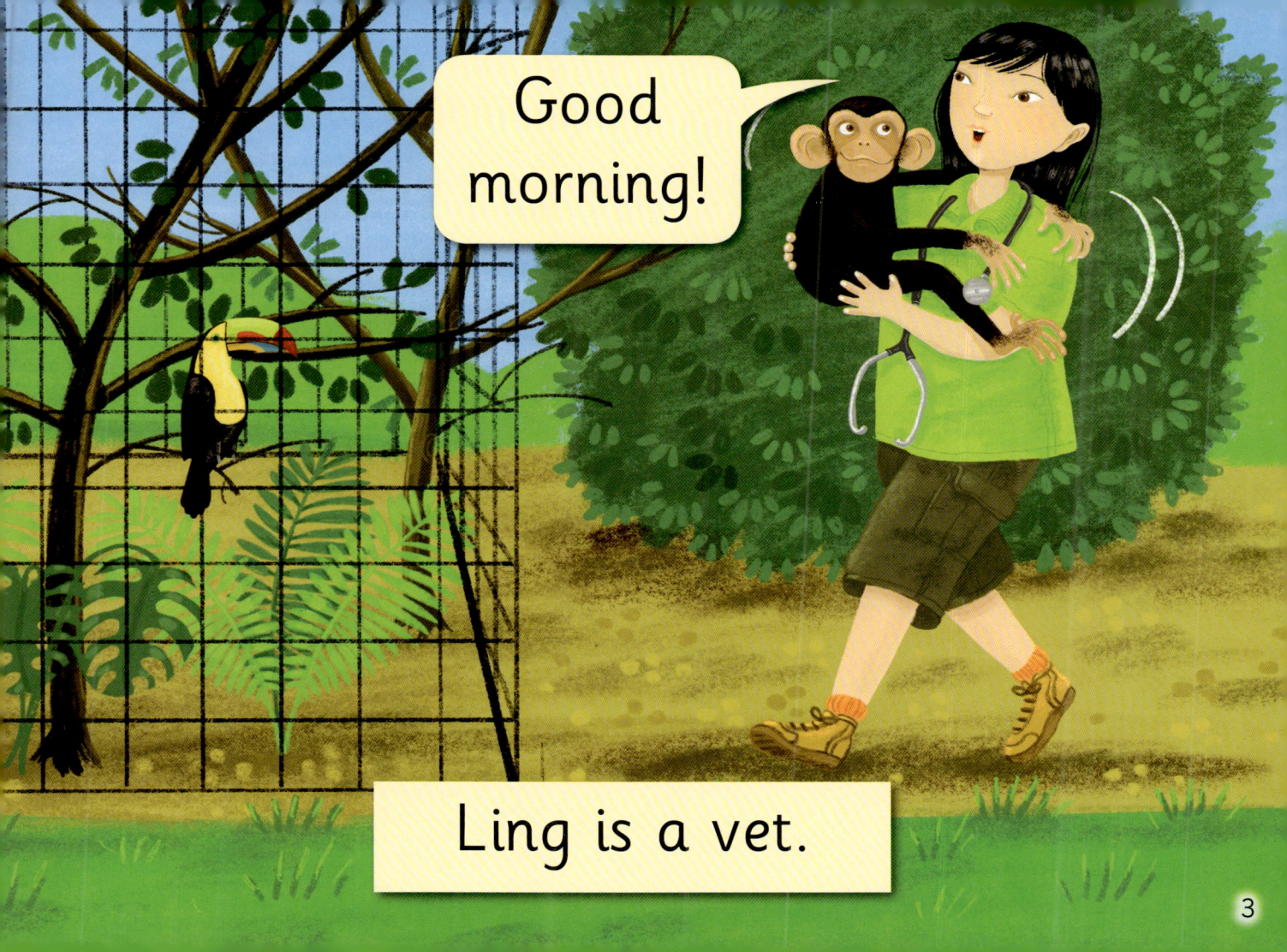

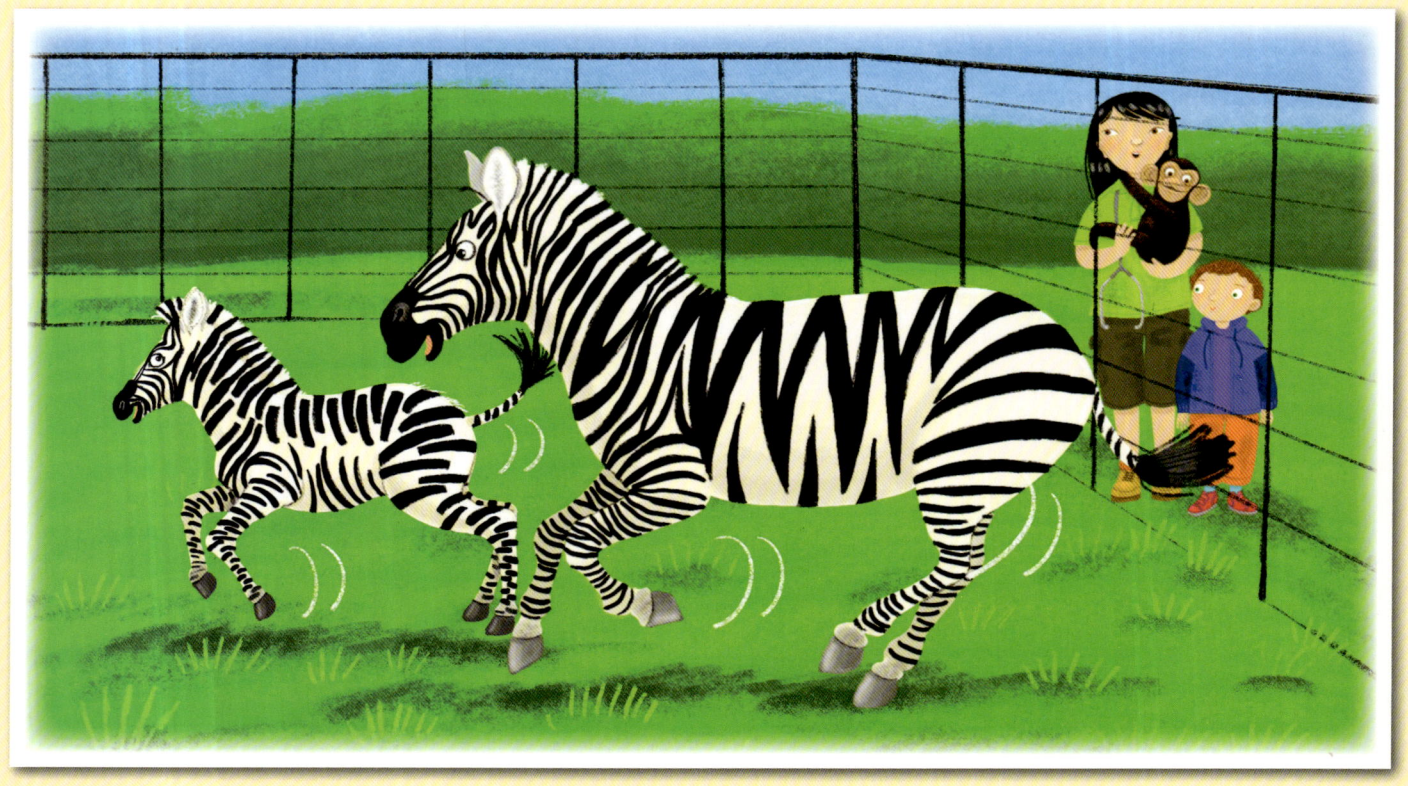

Zigzag and his foal, Zip, trot in a paddock.

Will helps Ling feed pelicans and raccoons.

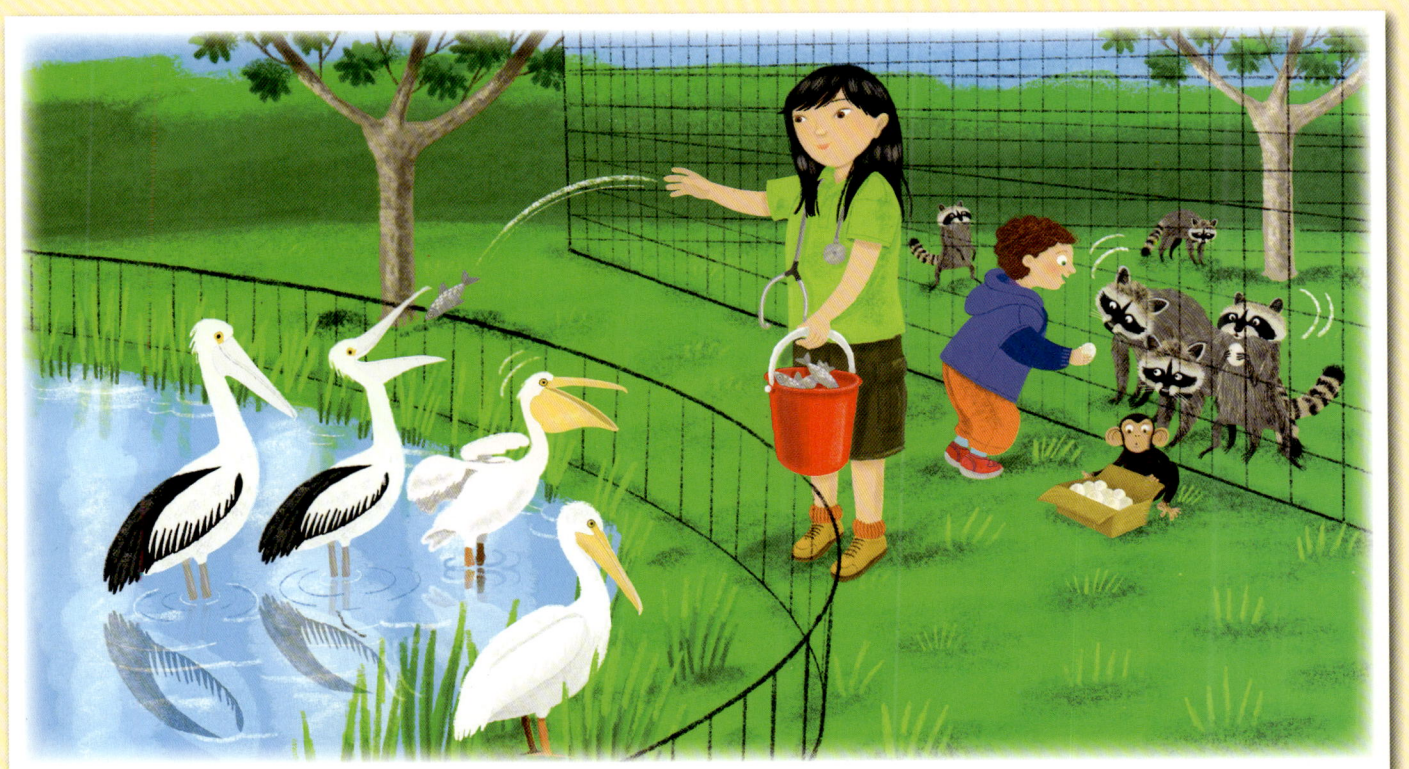

Boo unlocks a pen. Bad Boo!

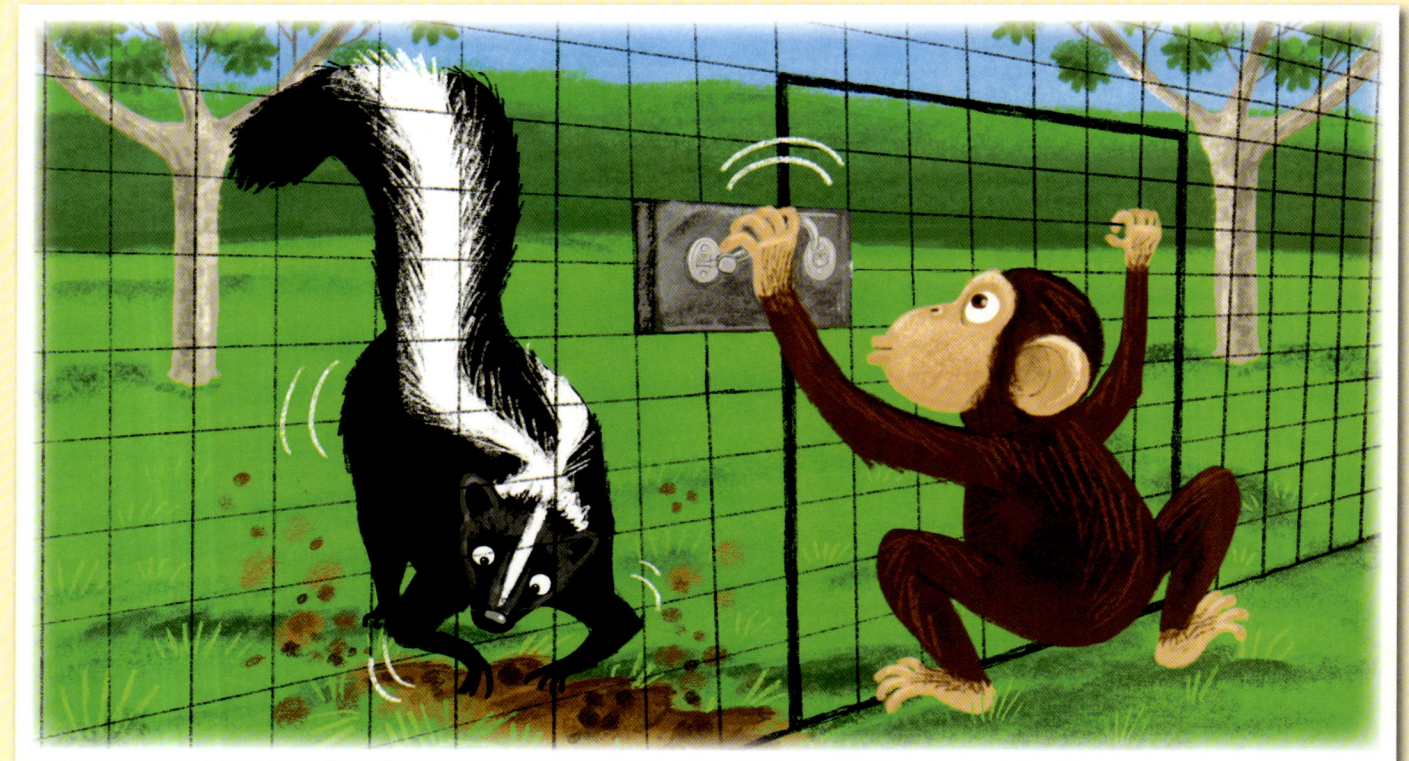

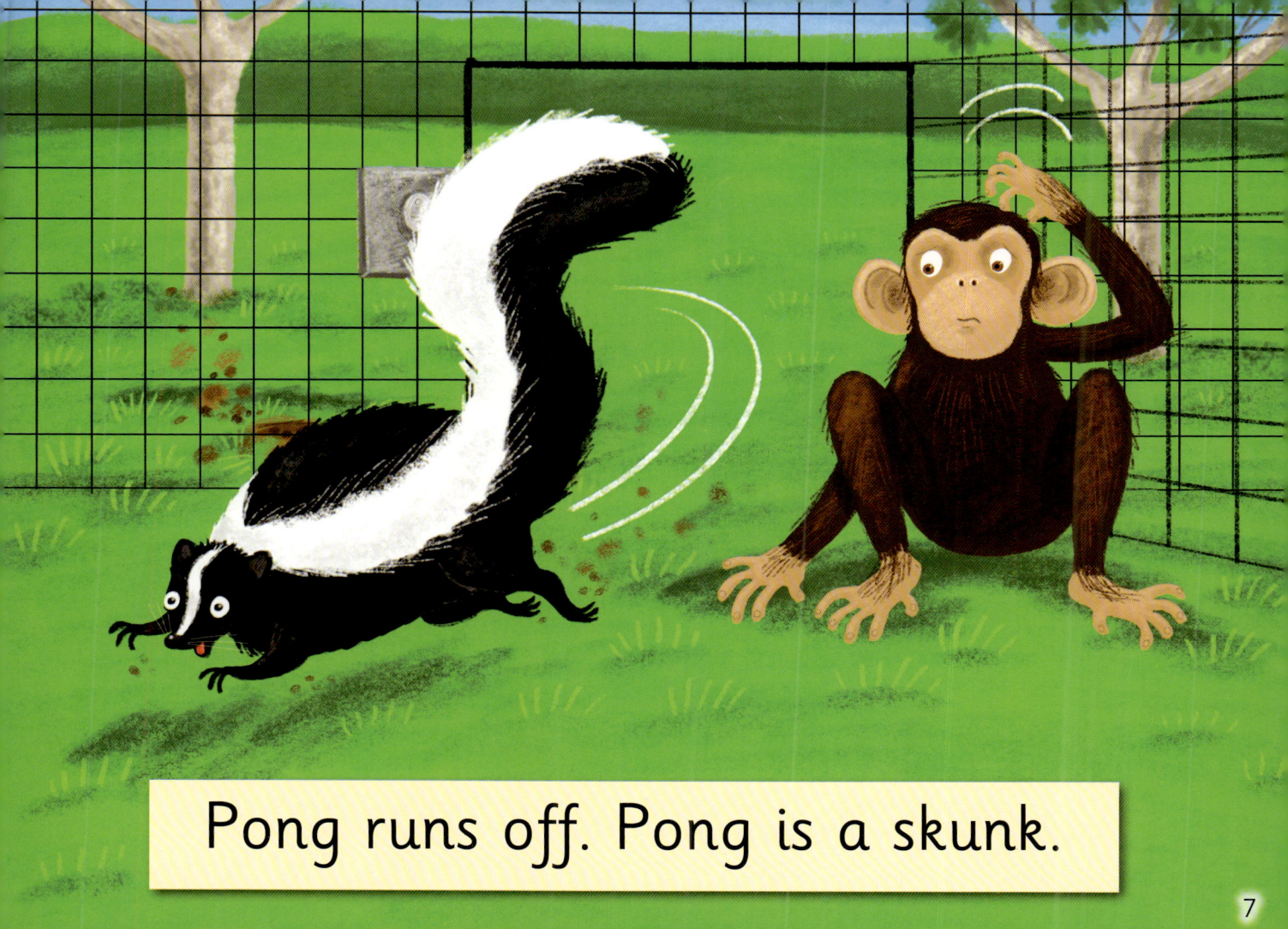

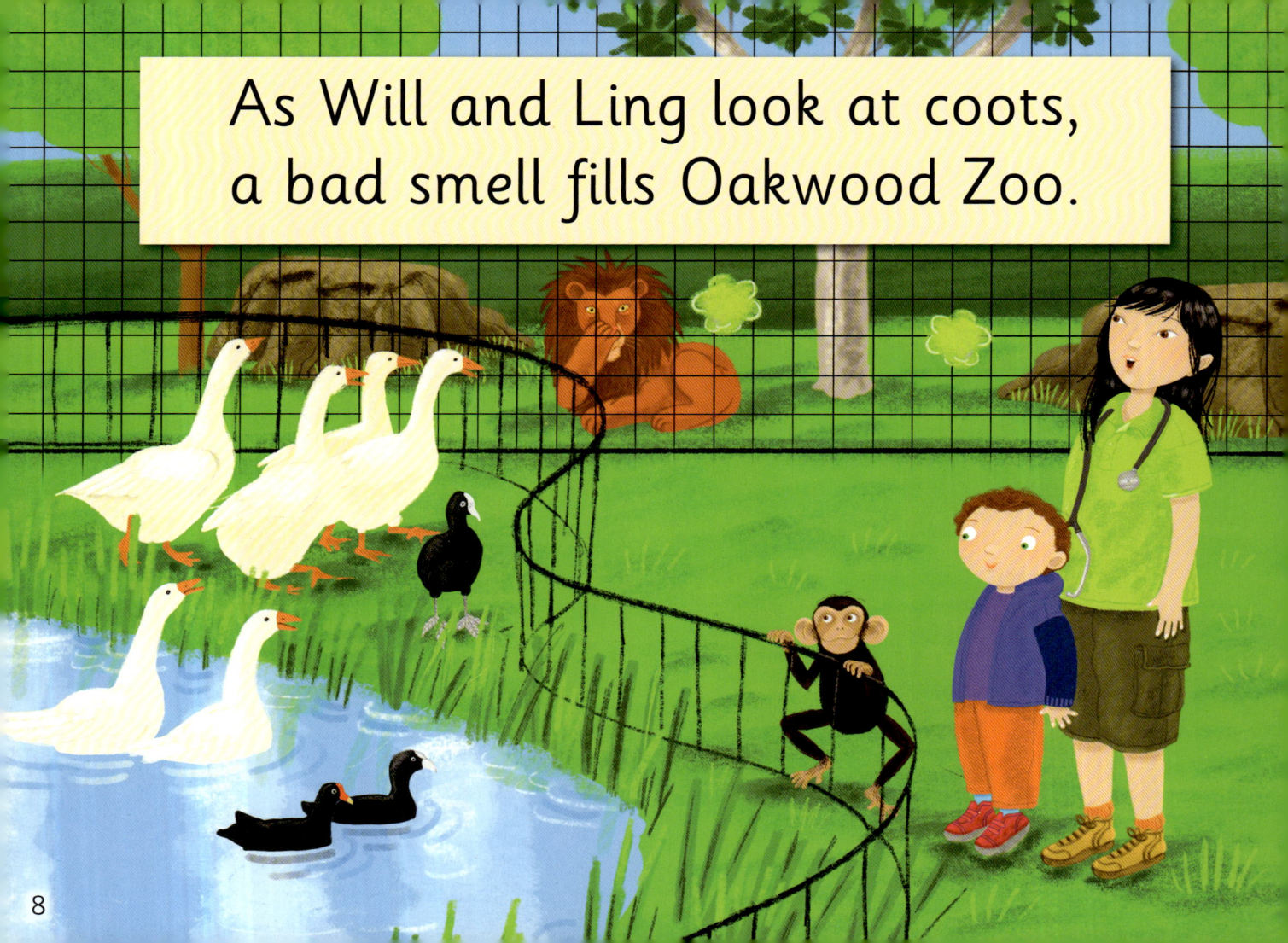
As Will and Ling look at coots, a bad smell fills Oakwood Zoo.

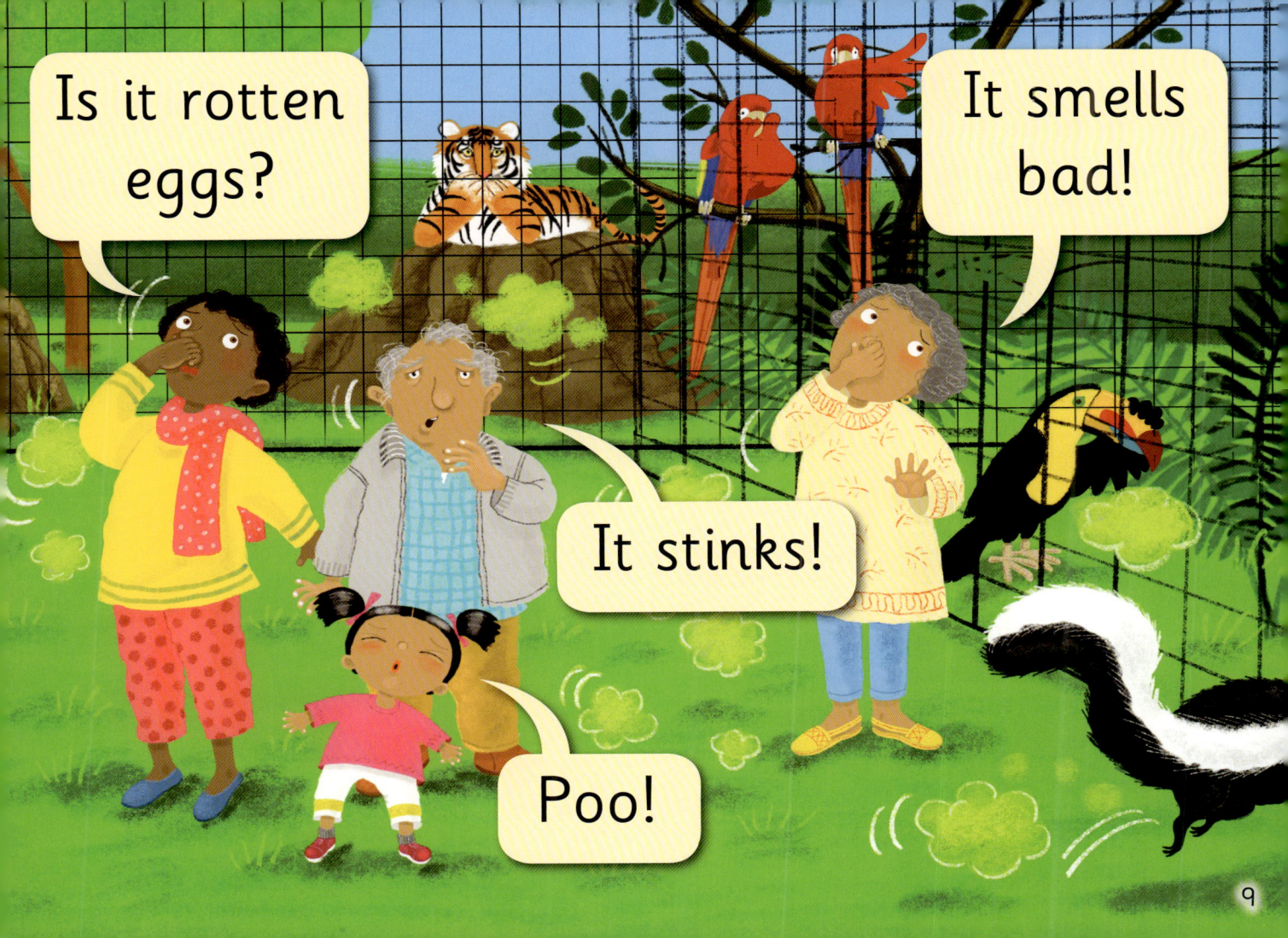

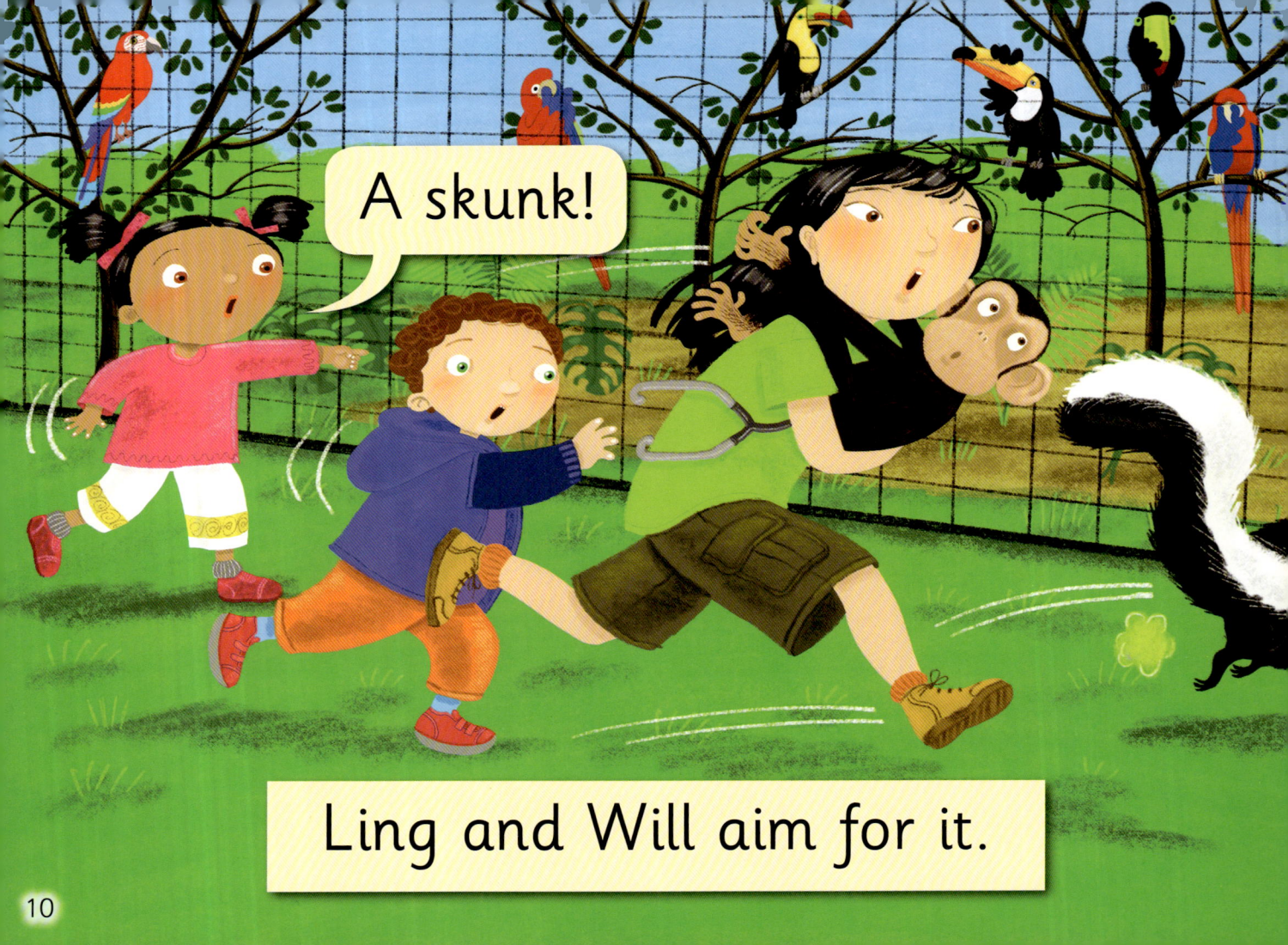

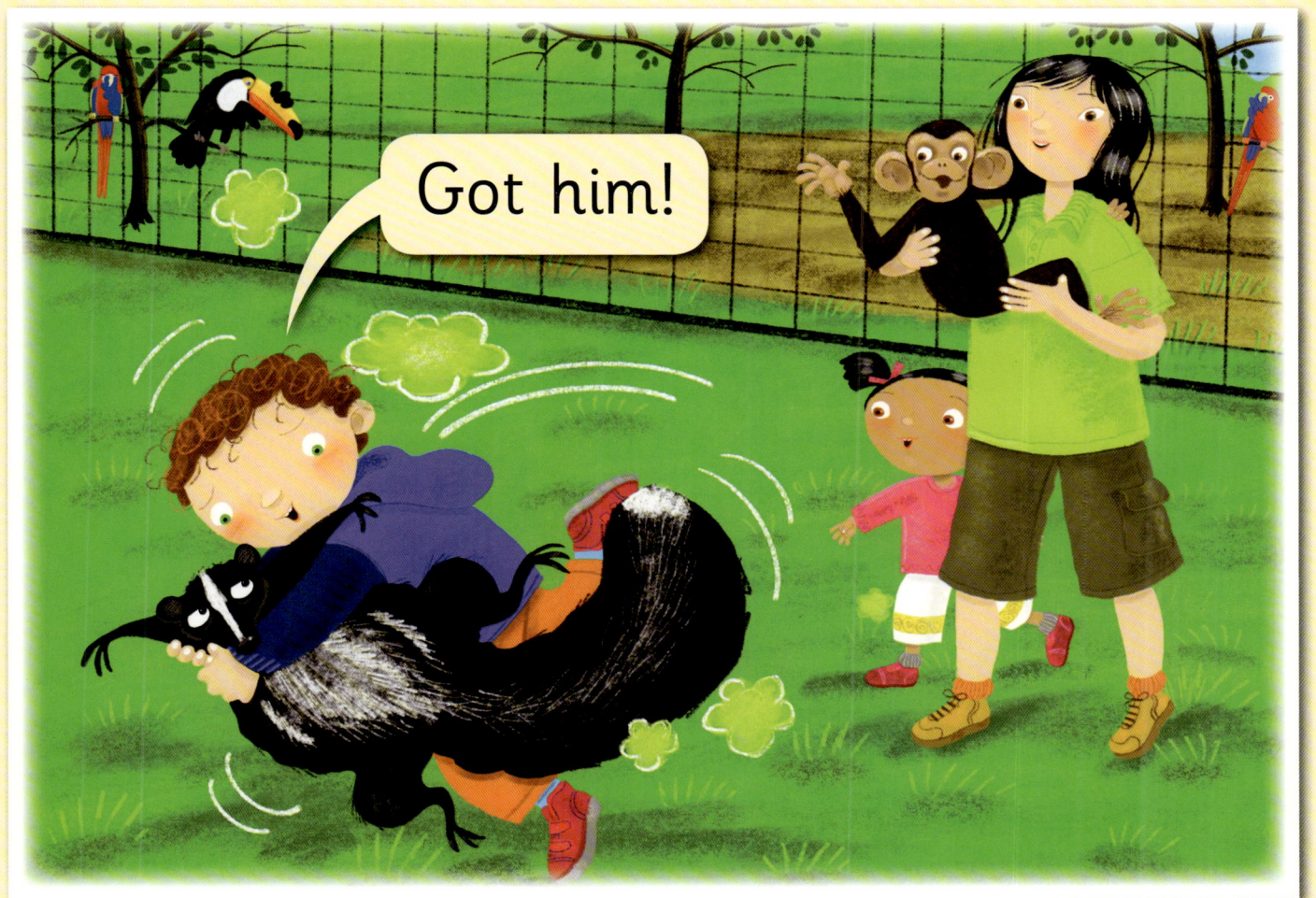

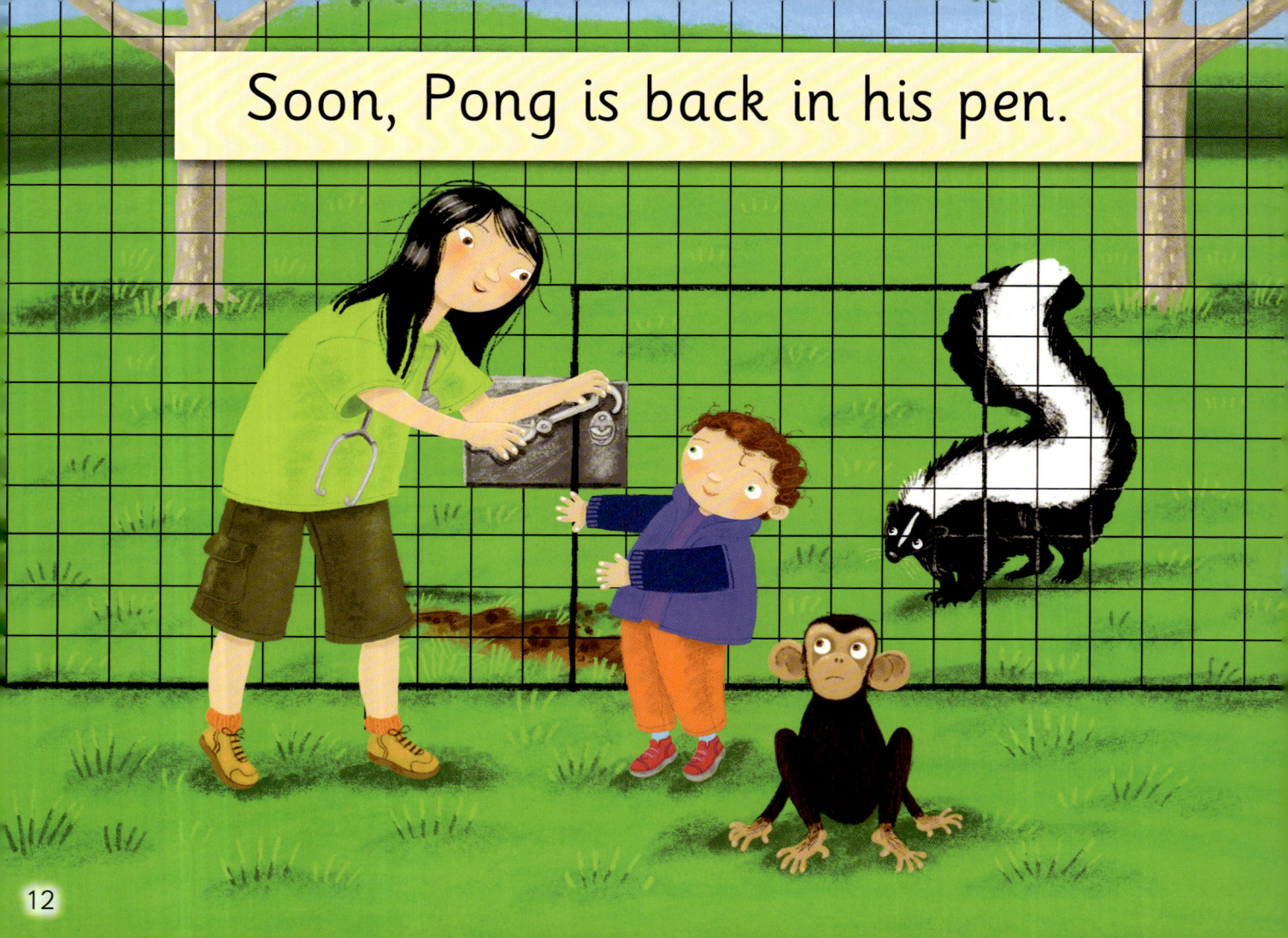
Soon, Pong is back in his pen.